AF430392

THE TOY

Parts 1 & 2

A Po Tale

CONTENTS

ISBN-13: 9798633559514
ISBN-10: 1477123456

Cover design by: Art Painter
Library of Congress Control Number: 2018675309
Printed in the United States of America

The Toy

It was just a whim. I had been shopping online for a gift for a friend. I wasn't able to find anything good, but a mood had struck and I found myself watching some porn. I was still on the shopping site, and out of curiosity I looked to see if they had any sex toys.

My wife and I occasionally include toys in our love life. Nothing too extreme. A vibrator once in a while, and a couple of vibrating eggs that have come in handy. Well the vibrator that we have has been getting tired, we've had it a few years now, and it was starting to run a little slower and use the batteries faster.

I glanced around until I found one very similar to the one that needed to be replaced. While I was at it, I picked out a couple other things. A small set of anal beads because they were 35 cents and I was curious. A textured glass dildo because an old friend had once told me hers was her favorite toy. Then I saw one exactly like the one that needed to be replaced. So I clicked on it went to the checkout and was done with my shopping.

A few days later the toys started coming in the mail. Of-course they wouldn't all come in one box. There was a few days where discreet brown packages were left in the mail box. I told my wife about it, and she laughed and blushed. But was happy with the replacement for her trusted toy, and we had an amazing time trying out the glass dildo. (that's another story)

I had told my friend Emma about it. Emma is one of my best and most trusted friends. We met a few years ago. She worked at the local coffee shop where I stop every morning for a coffee and a biscuit. Emma is gorgeous. A tall thin beauty with amazing eyes. Her long wild hair frames her face perfectly, and no matter what colour she dyes it, it always seems perfect. Her body is absolutely amazing as well. A true model of perfection. From her full round tits to her her flat tummy down past her perfect ass to long smooth legs. When we first met I would deliberately let other customers cut in front of me just so I could watch her longer.

Over the years we had grown close. What started as casual flirting had become a fast and trusting friendship. The flirting never stopped either. We always made sure that the other was aware of any relationships we had, and we played within the rules. My beautiful wife got to know Emma, and they laugh and flirt as well. Its even gone so far as sending each other naughty photos on text msg. but we also talk in depth about everything that comes to mind. Help each other with problems. Watch each others children , etc. A normal adult friendship with the added bonus of both of us being the same sort of horny. It was nice to be able to be honest about it. To be genuine, and not have to hide the naughty thoughts, or choke back the sexual comments.

I let Emma know when the toys came in the mail. I even gave her a little detail about how well the glass one worked out when we tried it. She laughed and explained that she no longer had any sort of toys. Evidently she had gotten rid of them when she divorced her first husband. I had offered to give her the extra one that I bought. There just wasn't a point in having two that were so similar, and after all, it was just a couple bucks and she could sure use it. She readily agreed to take it, and we made a plan to give it to her on the next day that she visited the house.

Time had passed, and we hadn't been able to visit. Between work and family and helping a friend through some tough times, neither of us had had a chance to relax, let alone take a couple hours to visit. We kept in touch via text. Nearly constantly we chit chatted about this and that. We would flirt to distract each other from the stress of the day. And basically just stay in touch all day.

Finally we had made arrangements to hang out for a while. The kids were going to play together in the back yard, whilst the adults hung out and had a drink inside the nice air conditioned house. It had been a real hot spring, and the A/C had been running overtime trying to keep the heat wave at bay.

I got an idea. About 20 minutes before Emma was to arrive I carefully hid a couple of video cameras in my room. One on the clothes hamper, and another over on the computer desk. I set them to record and went back downstairs. Emma arrived, and we got the kids set up playing with the sprinkler out back. Emma and I went inside and sat at the table to have a beer and catch up. It didn't take too long and the conversation turned sexual; as it often does when the two of us chat.

Acting as if I just remembered, I reminded Emma that she could grab that extra toy I had bought a few weeks prior. She smiled so big her eyes sparkled. And she asked me to grab it for her. "No it's ok, I'll stay down here and keep an eye on the kids." I said, and I gave her directions where to find it tucked into the nightstand cabinet. I also told her she could take her time. Relax. Even try it out of she wanted. It was her day off and she was allowed.

We both had a big laugh about it. But she headed upstairs as I went out back to smoke a cigarette and check on the kids.

My heart was beating in my chest so fiercely that I could feel it pulsing in my ears. My hands were shaking as I lit a camel and tried to slow my breathing. I asked myself over and over again if I was too obvious. Wondering if she would go through with it, or simply grab her new toy, tuck it in her purse and come right down to join me on the porch.

I finished my cigarette and there was no sign of Emma. My nerves were still on edge. My face was tingling a little with the anticipation. I lit another cigarette and tried to control my breathing. I was light headed and started to feel as if I would pass out. My dick was as hard as its ever had been. Pressing against my button fly, threatening to break through. I took a deep drag off my cigarette, made sure the kids were playing safely and headed inside.

I stopped at the fridge and grabbed myself a beer. I cracked it open and drank about half of it down in one smooth swallow. I was sweating from the heat outside. Looking out the window I was a little jealous of the kids having fun running through the sprinkler... laughing and playing. For a second I forgot about Emma. I just watched the kids play and enjoyed the moment. I knew the kids would probably grow up to have vague memories of this afternoon. It would blur together with every other afternoon of this summer and probably the next. But today is a day that I would remember forever. Watching them play brought me back down to earth.

I finished my beer. I realized that it went down too quick. Probably only took about 4 swallows and it was gone. I attributed it to the heat, shrugged my shoulders and tip-toed up the stairs as softly as I could. Daring not to step in the center of any step, but only on the outside. Trying to avoid a squeak. It took a few moments to get up the stairs. I thought about how long had it been since Emma went upstairs? 10, maybe 20 minutes? I had smoked two cigarettes, and had a beer... surely it had been 15 minutes? I tip-toed down the hall. Careful not to step on any of the toys that the kids had left laying. Made a mental note to talk to them about picking up when they're done playing.

My blood began to rise again as I neared the end of the hall. The door was shut and initially I couldn't hear a sound. I carefully listened near the door. Nothing. Sloooowly I leaned forward and pressed my ear against the door. I braced my hand against the door frame so I wouldn't make the door move at all. I didn't want to risk a noise. I listened for the telltale hum of a toy... a moan ... a whisper... anything. As a leaned there carefully trying not to breathe too hard I did hear something. I heard the rustling of cloth. Maybe clothing? Blankets? I closed my eyes and tried to imagine what was making the sound. Through the oak of the door I couldn't be sure what part of the room it was in, but it sounded like it was coming from the bed. I stood and listened and I heard the distinctive sound of the antique night-stand drawer opening and closing. And it struck me...

I hadn't mentioned the drawer to Emma. I had just let her know that the toy I had bought for her was in the bottom of the nightstand hidden amongst the t-shirts and whatnot that My wife keeps in there. The drawer was dedicated to my wife's toys. My mind raced as I realized that Emma was looking in that drawer. What was she doing? Why was she in there? My heart raced faster. I wasn't sure if I should be angry that she was in there, or embarrassed that she had seen all the secret little naughties that we keep in there, or if I should be turned on by it all. Of course we had talked about it. We had talked about everything. We had even gone into detail about this toy and that. So I decided I couldn't be mad. Nor could I be embarrassed. That left turned on. I felt my balls tighten as I leaned against the door. My face burned with my heartbeat. My pulse thumping in my chest, my ears, my fingertips, and especially my cock. I heard soft footsteps coming towards the door. As quietly as I could I turned and bounded for the stairs! I had just padded my bare feet onto the bamboo floor of the dining room when I heard my bedroom door open.

I ran my hands through my hair and did my best to look bored as she came down the stairs. I had stepped behind the island to wipe the counter, while truly I was hiding the raging erection that I hadn't had a chance to tuck into my belt.

Emma was trying to look bored as well. Her face was flushed. There was still sweat beaded on her neck. And as she passed by me I could smell the sex on her. She smiled at me. Her eyes spoke volumes. The shade was deep, and they were so liquid. I am sure I could've dove right into those eyes, swam a lap and hopped out. She just smiled and walked past me then stepped into the down-stairs bathroom.

I had finished mopping the counter by the time she came out. She had wiped the sweat from her neckline, touched up her makeup, and had a huge grin on her face. I considered giving her a look, but decided to just laughingly ask her what took so long. Her face blushed, and her eyes sparkled and she said "thank you. I needed that" she smiled even deeper when she said "it works pretty good. I'm gonna use the hell outta this thing!" we both laughed as the tension melted out of the room. I tossed her a cig-arette and we both went out for a smoke.

We sat and watched the kids play for an hour or so. Smoking cigarettes and talking. I couldn't keep my mind off of what had happened. What I had heard. Wondering what she had done? Did my cameras catch anything? Emma didn't bring it up, and I did my best to leave it alone. After a while we realized it was time for her to get her kid home. Her hubby would be home soon, and she had planned on making him dinner before he got home.

We had just finished packing up her daughters stuff and getting it loaded into the jeep when my wife got home. Another ten minutes was spent just so the girls could laugh and talk, and complain about having it be such a short visit, then, with child safely buckled into the back-seat Emma drove off for home.

Jane had had a difficult day at the office. She kicked her shoes off and vented to me about all the little things about her day that had been difficult. I did my best to listen and be supportive. To help with dinner, and to go through all the daily motions. All the while, thinking about those two cameras sitting in my room. Wondering. Hoping.

Finally, dinner was done. Jane had the kids set down in front of the TV, and she had put her feet up on the sofa to read from her book. I took the opportunity to steal away to the bedroom and see if I had any luck.

I grabbed both cameras from where they had been hidden. One was powered down. Not surprising after it had been on for so long. The other still had a power light on. I sat at the computer and looked at the camera that was still on. This camera had 3 hours of recording space on it, after it was full it would automatically power down. I glanced at my watch and did the math. It was AT LEAST 5 hours since I had pressed the record button and left the camera sitting on the hamper.

My heart sank. Either Emma had noticed it and stopped the recording, or something had gone wrong and it didn't record anything at all. I shrugged and plugged them both into the charge cords at the computer. It would take a few minutes for them to synch, and for them to charge up enough to for me to download the files and see what I had captured. I grabbed a cigarette and went downstairs. Wondering. Hoping. Curious. My blood began to boil again as I stood in the dark and smoked. That familiar pressure against my button fly reminding me of Emma's smile as she came down the stairs. The smell of her as she passed me by on the way to the bathroom.

End part one.

The Toy 2

A Gift Received, and Given

Poe was a great friend. We met at my work, I am a Barista at a small coffee stand. He came in nearly every morning for a cup of coffee and a breakfast bun. He's a great looking guy, not too tall, not too muscular, but with a definite confidence in the way he carries himself. His walk, his smile, and especially his eyes are confident. He is a man that knows what he wants, and knows just what he'll do next.

At first I just appreciated him for what it was. A good looking guy that came through my line. But as time passed, I noticed myself thinking of him as I did my morning make-up. Even watching the clock and waiting for the time that he usually arrived. On days that he didn't come in because He was off work, or running late, I was always a little let down. He has a way of looking at me that absolutely melts me, and often gets me wet just from his stare.

Sometimes it seemed he would drag his feet so he would be the last person in my line. His eyes and his voice always made my whole day. His eyes are an amazing hazel blend. I could tell by the colour of them how he was feeling. When he was tired they were very brown. A rich deep brown. When he was happy they were nearly emerald green, with gold sparkles around the outside.

His voice was something out of a romance novel. Deep baritone, but raised in pitch if he was excited about something. He was animated when he was excited. Talking with his hands, and his eyes sparkling to accent his points. His whole body became part of the conversation. I often wondered in those first few weeks what he looked like under his work clothes. He carried himself with confidence and a devil-may-care attitude. He had a style that was all his own. From his haircut to his loose fitting jeans with extra wallet chains. Here was a man that lived on his terms… and No-one else's.

We became friends over time. At first it was casual flirting at the register, then we exchanged numbers and stayed up all night long texting. He was married (of course) and he was very sure to tell me that he was not a cheating man. I still find him to be one of the most attractive men I have ever met.

We had known each other for a few years, and become the best of friends. I could talk to Poe about absolutely everything. We talked about parenting, relationships, art, music, life in general, and sex. Somehow we always wound up talking about sex. I could and often would confide in him about my sexual frustrations with my boyfriend. His wife was an absolute peach, beautiful and smart. But she didn't treat him the way he deserved. He never seemed to notice or care. He would just go through life with that intoxicating smile. Never wavering. Poe and I had been having a particularly steamy text conversation one night. I guess he was shopping for some new sex toys to use, and He and I talked about all the things he had tried, all the things I had tried, and just which ones were the best. He even jokingly said that he had accidentally ordered one too many. I had gotten rid of all of my toys when my marriage ended a few years back. I always meant to go buy something, to treat myself. But My Jim wasn't a fan of toys, he said they were "cheating". So I made do with what I had. My fingers, and occasionally a back massager that My mother had gotten me for Christmas. I don't need to tell you that after Poe and I stopped talking that night, I spent a good hour with that massager. And it never touched my back!

Things had gotten hectic for a while, and I wasn't able to see him much aside from the morning routine at work. A mutual friend of our was going through a rough time, and he and I were taking turns helping out. Eventually things settled back into their regular groove and Poe and I made a play date for the kids to get together.

I always love our "play dates" Poe would rush about and get his place all cleaned up before me and my daughter would arrive. It always smelled of fresh pine-sol, and the grass was always freshly cut. He always tried to play it off like He had just done his regular chores. But with the sweat still beading on his forehead, I could tell that he was going the extra mile for my benefit. And I liked it. It felt good to be appreciated like that, by a man like that. A man that wasn't afraid to be in control of his environment. He was able to set the scene every time we came over.

Usually we would set the kids up to play, either outside on a swing set he had built, or in the kids room with dolls, or sometimes just the latest Disney movie. Once the kids were all set, we would sit and chat for hours. Talk about all the things that had happened in our lives, gossip about the local goings-on, and just catch up. I loved how he payed attention to me. I could tell that he listened to every word I said. And I waited patiently to hear his. The best and most intimate conversations were had at his dining table while the kids played. We would often talk about sex too, which was one of my favourites. I wondered if he knew how many times I raced straight home from his house to take care of myself. Thinking about those eyes, piercing into me, or his strong hands wrapped around my waist. He was a working man, and though he was careful to keep his hands clean and his nails clipped. He had strong hands. I had seen him move things that were far too heavy for me to even lift, with a casual ease, as if size and weight was of no importance to him. I dreamed of those hands, those arms, those fingers, those lips. The muscles of his back, off his chest, the strength of his core. I wondered what it would feel like to have his body against mine. Glistened in sweat. I wondered if he would toss me around with the ready ease that he tossed around those bricks in the yard.

It had been a very hot spring time. Temperatures were setting records all over the state. My AC had conked out, and there weren't any available in the stores. Sold out for weeks. Poe had invited my daughter and I over for a play date. Said the kids could play in the sprinkler, and we could hang out in his Air conditioned kitchen. Of-course I readily agreed.

Things at home had been tough. With no AC my Boyfriend Jim had been especially cranky. I wasn't getting the house work done to his standard, and he was just a bear to be around in general. There was no relief at night either. It was over 80f even in the night. Fans in the windows would make it possible to just barely sleep enough to function. There was just no way we were going to have any sex. Between the temperatures and the attitudes... it just hadn't happened.

We arrived at Poe and Janes house around mid day. It was already unbearable hot out. He greeted us at the door as he always did. I could tell that he made no exception to his pre-visit routine. His hands and face were freshly washed, but his neck showed beads of sweat, and his shoes had fresh cut grass on the toes. He greeted us with hugs, first my daughter, then me. Did he linger longer than usual? Was he wearing a new after-shave? We came in to the Climate controlled house and it felt AMAZING. He kept it at around 65f during the summer. It was at first a little too cold, but it was soo refreshing.

We got the kids set up in their swim suits, slathered them in SPF 10,000 and turned them loose on the back yard sprinkler. They were laughing and playing in no time. Making up games and shrieking with glee. It made me miss the days of summer when I was a little girl.

Poe and I sat at the table and chatted over coffee. It felt so good to be cooled off. The house smelled amazing. I could tell that he had swept and mopped. The scent of pine was still faint in the air. There was also incense burning near the kitchen window. So it was circulated through the room by the Cool AC air. I sat across from this man. My closest and dearest friend, and also the sexiest man I had ever known. It just oozed out of him. I knew he didn't try. Somehow his white t-shirt clung to him in just the right places. His faded weekend Levis, were worn in just the right places. His voice filled the room just enough to leave me feeling empty after he finished his sentence. From across the table I could just make out the smell of his after shave. When he stood to refill my cup, I caught myself staring directly at the bulge in his pants.

We had been friends for a few years now. Talked about everything under the sun. I had sent him countless sexy photos asking his opinion of how I looked, and sometimes just to get the confidence boost. But He had never shown me anything beyond what I might see at the beach. He was a good husband and father. The fact that he held to his morals was soo sexy.

It had been so hot that I hadn't bothered with my regular underwire bra. I had just thrown on a sports bra and a light tank top. On the bottom I was wearing a thong and my favourite black leggings. Anything to beat the infernal heat. As I sat there in the cool air conditioned room, staring at this mans crotch, I felt my nipples standing proud and rubbing against the sports bra. I don't know if he noticed. IF he did he sure didn't let on. He just kept up his side of the conversation, smiling all the while with his care-free smile. His eyes glinting green and gold in the sunlight. Eventually(as it often did) the conversation turned towards sex.

I lied and said that my sex life had been average for the past few weeks. In honesty I think it had been nearly a month since Jim had taken me. And before that it had only been quickies before or after work. Trying to take advantage of what time we could afford between busy schedules. As Poe talked, I could feel my nipples getting so hard that they started to hurt. That good hurt. It made me feel sexy. Sexier than I had felt in a long time. My pussy was getting wet. To the point I was SURE that I had soaked through my thong, and was wondering if my black leggings were going to hide the wet spot at my crotch. Poe commented that he was getting a bit jittery from all the coffee and offered to grab us each a cold beer. I readily accepted.

As he walked out to the garage fridge for beers, I took a moment to check on the kids. As I walked to the back door, I felt that my pussy was so wet it was slipping against my underwear. I glanced over my shoulder to see if Poe was watching. With him out of sight I chanced a quick touch. My leggings were soaked through! I had to find a way to keep that hidden! I tugged down the front of my tank top. It would barely cover my crotch as long as I didn't stretch or lean back. With a sigh of relief, I peeked on the kids. They were still playing with abandon. Jumping through the ice cold sprinkler, and running through the yard. Looked like some sort of tag. Laughter filled the back yard.

I got sat back down, just as Poe returned with 2 frosty cold beers. He sat down across from me, and after opening both beers, slid a bottle across the table for me. It felt great on my throat. Even with the AC I was starting to sweat a bit. The cold beer was refreshing, and helped to cool me down. But did nothing to quench the fire in my pants. The feel of the hard bottle in my hands, the smooth glass against my lips. Poe's eyes on mine. It all just fueled the fire in my pussy. I was squirming in my seat. Doing my best not to let him notice. Afraid that he'd call me out for being such a horn-dog.

I couldn't help myself, and before I realized I was doing it, I had one hand under the table, casually toying with my pussy through my leggings. Not too hard, just running my finger over the hot and slippery material. I was so wet that my leggings were saturated. Slightly and lightly touching my hood, tracing my lips. It was sending tingles all the way to my toes just to have the light touch. Poe hadn't noticed. He was still talking about how he had upgraded his toy collection that night. Telling me about how that lucky bitch of a wife of his enjoyed it when he used the toys on her.

As He spoke. His voice so smooth and warm, I pressed harder onto my labia. The pressure felt wonderful. I was working myself into a bit of a frenzy. I was about to excuse myself and go finger myself properly in the bathroom when Poe said. "oh yeah, speaking of which, I did end up ordering one too many of those vibrators. You can still have the spare one if you want it." I nearly fainted when he mentioned that there was a vibrator FOR ME in the house. I collected myself, and tried not to sound too excited.

"Sure Hon, why don't you grab it for me?" Thinking that he would grab it, and I would pretend to put it in my purse, then discreetly sneak off to the bathroom and give myself a good fucking.

"Nah, It's my turn to check on the kids. Why don't you just grab it… its in the lower cabinet of the nightstand in my room…" Then he spoke again, "No rush either. It's your day off, take your time, heck, even try it out if you want."

I couldn't believe my ears! Had this man, just offered to let me masturbate on his bed? In his room? While he watched my daughter? Of-course there was absolutely no way I would do such a thing. But he said it soo nonchalant. Like it was nothing at all. "oh go ahead and fuck yourself on my sheets, no biggie…"

I was so flustered that I couldn't think of a way to decline and have him go get it for me. There was no way that I could walk past him to go check on the kids myself. He would definitely see how wet I was. As it was I was positive that he could see my nipples pressing hard against the back of my top. I could feel every breath causing the material to rub on them. Every heartbeat was pulsing directly in my pussy. He shrugged as if his prior statement was nothing at all, and he stood and walked to the sliding glass door to check on the kids.

I made my escape! I quickly stood and rushed towards the stairs. My legs were weak and knees a little shaky as I bounded up the steps and out of his sight. How embarrassed would I be if he saw me in this state? Nipples so hard that my tits were just aching to be touched. Pussy so wet that there was a visible wet spot not just on my crotch, but starting to get onto the thighs and ass of my leggings.

His bedroom was at the end of the hall. I coved the length of the hallway in just a few long strides. Opened the door, stepped in, and locked it behind me. As soon as the lock "clicked" one had shot up my shirt and under my bra, the other went straight into my panties. I rubbed my tits hard. Trying to calm them. But as I slid my other hand into my panties, and felt just how soaked my pussy was, I could help but to put first 1, then 2 fingers right up my pussy. My left hand went from rubbing my tit, to pinching my nipple.

I was in trouble.

Before things got any worse, I decided to slip out of my leggings. At least maybe they could dry a bit. I bent at the waist and slid the leggings over my hips. As I worked to get the legs pulled past my feet I glanced at the clothes hamper. Maybe I could put my leggings into his laundry and "borrow" a pair of Janes? We were about the same size, and after all. Black leggings are pretty common right? Any thought of clothing was over ruled by the immediacy of my pussy. I kicked the leggings towards the hamper, sat on the edge of the bed and gave in to myself. I quickly pulled the crotch of my thong panty to the side for better access and started rubbing my clitty.

Usually I like to tease myself a while, and make sure that I am good and wet when I masturbate. Not today. I was so horny that my breath was coming in gasps. I rubbed my clit as hard and as fast as I could. At first just one hand, then I used the other hand to pull my hood back. I laid back on Poe's bed. Lost in my passion. One, tow, three fingers pistoning in and out of my pussy, while I rubbed my clit with my other hand. It was fast. Passionate. Furious. It only took me about 2 minutes of this treatment and I could feel the pressure building. It came over me like a wave. I felt it start at my toes, in my hair, in my fingertips... it started as tingle, then turned to a warmth that flowed over me as if someone was pouring water on me. I felt my face go flush, and I could barely breathe.

Just as I was about to cum, I slipped one finger out of my pussy and shoved it into my tight asshole as the other two went back into my pussy. And that's all it took. With tow fingers in my pussy and one in my ass. My other hand rubbing my clit, I came. And boy did I cum. It flowed through me. I could feel it pulsing, throbbing with my heartbeat. I could feel my pussy and ass spasm on my fingers, getting tighter and looser with the beating of my heart.

I laid there for a moment, catching my breath, before I remembered just where I was. What had I just Done!? I just fingered myself in my best friends bed! Sure he is the epitome of good looking, and good lord he's sexy... but its still HIS bed! Where his wife sleeps! Embarrassed I was going to grab my leggings and run right out of the house. Then I realized why it was that I had come up here in the first place. To grab a vibrator. That Poe himself had bought for me. That he had told his wife he would give to me. I giggled at my silliness and rolled on the bed to get my new toy.

In the bottom of the night stand there was a collection of old white shirts. Poe had told me that he and Jane used these for "clean-up" in the bedroom. So I grabbed one and mopped up some of my wetness from my crotch and thighs. Laying on my stomach, with one hand covered in an old t-shirt, mopping at my soaking wet pussy, I found the toy. It was about 6 or 7 inches long. Standard torpedo shaped vibrator. It was a bright purple. I sat up and fiddled with the packaging So I could take it out and look at it closer. It took me a while but I managed to get the plastic package open enough to slide the toy out. It was incredibly smooth. Had a decent weight to it. There was a twist knob at the tail end to turn it on. I twisted it. Nothing. Opened it up... No batteries. *sigh*

I glanced around the room, wondering where Poe might keep a couple AA batteries. TV stand? No. Dressers? No... Computer desk? Maybe... I stood to walk to the desk. As I stood, I shed my soaked thong, letting it fall to the floor near my leggings between the bed and the hamper.

Glancing at the desk top on the computer desk I didn't see any batteries. So I looked up to the top shelf, wondering if there might be some there. And I saw it.

A small video camera. Pointed right at the bed. Sitting on top of the computer desk. There was a small red light on. I grabbed it and turned it around. The view finder was on, and I could see the red record symbol in the corner. I pressed the stop button. Rewound it, pressed play. At first it was just the bed. Nothing moving. I cued it forward until I saw movement, and there it was... a video of me. From the moment I walked into the room until I was laying back and fingering myself like a porn star on the bed. At first I Was mad... there was a heat building in my stomach. Rage, embarrassment, outrage... how could he trap me with a hidden camera?

But as I watched myself on camera, I began thinking of Poe watching me on camera. I thought of him jerking his huge cock while staring at me on video. I started to see how sexy I looked in the video. I could feel my pussy getting wet again. As

I watched the video, I realized how the angle wasn't perfect. A lot of the "action" was obscured. Without thinking I had sat back on the bed. Now naked from the waist down. Then I had an idea.

I set the camera down and checked the drawer of Janes nightstand. The one that had held my toy and the now dorky t-shirt. JACKPOT there were all of Janes sex toys. Dildo's and vibrators, and anal beads. Most importantly: a package of new AA batteries!

I turned Poe's camera back on. Then went and set it on the TV stand. I was careful to aim it at the bed in a way that wouldn't let him see EVERYTHING. I pulled off my shirt and sports bra, glanced to the door to be sure it was till closed and locked, and I pressed record on the camera.

Heat traveled through my body. I could feel my pulse, beating in my ears, in my chest, and in my pussy. My nipples were rock hard again as I sat on the bed. I made direct eye contact with the camera. I smiled and gave Poe one of me sexiest winks. Then I got on all fours and reached into the toy drawer. I grabbed 2 fresh batteries, and put them into my new toy. I glanced over my shoulder as I turned it on. At first I rubbed in over my ass cheeks, it felt amazing! This was a strong one! It vibrated hard enough that I could clearly feel it in my pussy even from my ass cheek!

I rolled over and spread my legs. Again looking right at the camera. I was a little scared, but I kept going. I closed my eyes and played the vibrator over my aching nipples. I first one side then the other, I circled my areola and then pressed the vibrating tip into my nipples. I was so horny that my areola were shrunk up tight and my nipples were standing proud as gumdrops.

I put my head back, and let the toy trail down my chest, down my stomach, and finally get to my thighs. I teased myself for a few moments, before I pressed it against my clit. I came right away. I could feel my pussy pulsing and felt a little cum drip out and run into my ass crack. I was nowhere near done. I plunged it in. all the way. It filled me nicely. And I loved the feel of it vibrating inside me. I worked it in and out for a while... then pulled it out and held it to my clit. Then back inside... I would almost cum from it being inside me, then almost cum from it being on my clit... If only it could be in 2 places at once.

Unless???

I rolled back over and went back to the drawer. There was another vibrator just like the one I was using. I grabbed it and tossed it on the bed. I also grabbed a little chrome vibrating egg. I used to have one just like it, and it had been one of my favourites. I twisted the power dial on the vibe… it was good. Then found the switch on the cord of the egg. It was good also… So I gathered up all three toys and laid back on the bed. I took a moment to make sure that I was aimed right at the camera… If I was going to do this, I wanted to be SURE that this man got a good show.

The idea of Poe watching me started to overtake my thoughts again… My mouth was getting dry as I got started. I started where I had left off… with one toy against my clit. Then I grabbed the other vibrator and held it against my lips. The added vibrations felt amazing. My pussy and ass tightened up and I could feel that building sensation deep in my core. I pushed the vibrator into my pussy and held the other on my clit… my pussy lit up with electricity!

It felt so amazing. Without moving either toy, I could just flex my pussy muscles and it felt amazing. I tried to relax, and let go of the one in my pussy. Good it stayed…. I reached and grabbed the chrome egg. First I looked it right at the camera, and I brought it up to my mouth. I put it in my mouth and sucked on it, making sure to get it covered in spit. Then I reached behind my thigh and brought it to my ass. I relaxed, and pushed out a bit, and it started to slide in. I hadn't had anything bigger than a finger in my ass for quite some time, but this toy slid in without much resistance at all. I felt it push past the ring and fall into place inside me. The vibrator in my pussy had fallen out during the push and was buzzing on the mattress. I left it lay there and followed the wire from my ass to the controller. With a "click" the egg turned on. At first it was a very slow vibration, almost a rumble. As I turned the dial it intensified. I turned it all the way up. With my ass vibrating at full speed and my clit still under attack from my left hand, I looked again to the camera. I blew Poe a kiss as I picked up the second vibrator. I plunged it into my gaping pussy. It was all too much. It felt better than anything I had ever felt! I stroked in and out of my pussy a few times, and I started to cum.

I pulled the vibe out of my pussy, and the other off of my clit. I arched my back and let it wash over me. It began somewhere deep. Somewhere unknown, somewhere we only access at just the right moment. But as I lay there covered in sweat, I felt the orgasm building. I clenched my jaw against screaming. I writhed on the bed lifting my hips to be fucked by a man that wasn't there. Imagining Poe pistoning into me... imagining his cock in my moth and my pussy and my ass all at once. That was it. I felt it rush through me. I felt my come actually spurt out of me. I felt the cool air of the room reach into my pussy as it opened and closed of its own accord. I turned my head and bit into the pillow to keep from crying out. That egg... taking me over the edge and beyond. The other toys lost, I grabbed a breast in each hand and tore at my nipples as I rode the plateau of this orgasm. A few moments of this felt like an eternity. I couldn't take it anymore, but I needed it to stop... I tried to breathe, I tried to swallow... My entire body tingling in pins and needles. My pussy still vibrating from the egg up my ass. I reached over and shut off the egg. And laid back to catch my breath.

A few moments passed before I again remembered my situation. I pulled the egg out, and wiped it on the shirt from before, wiping my soaking pussy. There was a small puddle on the sheet. I sat up and rubbed at it with the shirt, that was now too wet to be of any use. I rolled and grabbed another from the night stand cabinet. I wiped the sweat from my tits, and armpits, then did my best to clean the spot off the sheet. I wiped down the egg again, as well as Jane's purple vibrator. I sucked mine clean, wiped it and put it back into its packaging.

As I was putting Janes toys away in the drawer I heard the door move in its frame. I froze! I stayed absolutely still and silent. Listening to the beating of my heart. Nothing. Maybe the wind? I hurriedly closed the drawer, making sure that everything was as I found it. Then grabbed the camera and hit the "stop" button. I considered for a moment deleting it. But before I could talk myself out of it, I placed the camera back on the computer desk as I had found it.

I went to my pile of clothes near the hamper. Slid on my panties that dried enough to be slightly stiff from my dried wetness. Slid on my leggings that seemed to be ok. As I reached for my sports bra, I saw another camera. Sitting atop the laundry hamper, there it was. Another small camera, with another small red light.

I laughed to myself about not expecting it from Poe. He had told me multiple times how he liked to hide cameras in the bedroom and occasionally the bathroom to catch Jane in the act. I shook my head as I finished dressing. Before leaving the room, I looked right into the hamper camera, held the new toy up to my lips and kissed the package. "Thank you Poe, I needed that. I hope we can keep this our little secret," I spoke softly.

I blew another kiss towards the camera and made my way down the stairs. I had no idea how long I had been up there. Could've been 10 minutes, could've been 2 hours. As I came down the stairs I saw Poe standing behind the counter wiping the countertop that had been spotless when I arrived. I stepped a little closer to him on my way to the bathroom and noticed that his dick was pressing hard against the fly of his jeans. He mumbled something past his million dollar smile, "Thanks, Poe! I needed that!" I said, smiling. I dropped my new toy into my purse at the table and I went to the bathroom to clean up.

After a washcloth cleanup in the bathroom, I composed myself and went back out to finish our visit. Poe made no more comments about the toy, or how long I had been upstairs. We watched the kids play, enjoyed each others company. Eventually Jane came home. I liked her, but was always a little jealous of her for having such a great man, and not treating him like I felt he should be treated. We made friendly small talk until it was time for me to take my daughter home for supper. To brave the heat for another night with no AC.

I slept better that night than I had in months!

ABOUT THE AUTHOR

A Po Tale

"Po" is the pseudonym of an American author that prefers to remain nameless and al-
low his readers to create their own illusions
and fantasies.

West Coast born during the Reagan admin-
istration, Po was raised in multiple locations across the USA. Evident in his writing
style, that lends itself to multiple geographical locations, as well
as evidencing an open minded view not obstructed by any par-
ticular cultural norm.

From the foggy mornings of the pacific northwest, to the sunny
afternoons of southern California, or the freezing winters of the
lake superior region. Po's stories are written so they can be ap-
plied to the readers own imagination. In hopes that the reader can
transport themselves to a realm of fantasy and relaxation. Un-
burdened with the stress of daily routine.

Whether taking a break from work, enjoying a comfortable read
in the bath, or just passing the time during the day or night. It is
the hope of the author that you the reader are able to escape into
a story. If only just for a short while.